Me and Nana

by
Leslie Kimmelman

Pictures by
Marilee Robin Burton

Harper & Row, Publishers

Me and Nana
Text copyright © 1990 by Leslie A. Kimmelman
Illustrations copyright © 1990 by Marilee Robin Burton
Printed in the U.S.A. All rights reserved.
1 2 3 4 5 6 7 8 9 10
First Edition

Library of Congress Cataloging-in-Publication Data
Kimmelman, Leslie.
    Me and Nana / written by Leslie Kimmelman ; illustrated by Marilee
Robin Burton.
        p.   cm.
    Summary: Natalie's fun-filled activities with her grandmother
include shopping, going to the zoo, having snacks, and feeding the
dogs in the neighborhood.
    ISBN 0-06-023166-1 : $. — ISBN 0-06-023163-7 (lib. bdg.) :
$
    [1. Grandmothers—Fiction.]   I. Burton, Marilee Robin, ill.
II. Title.
PZ7. K56493Me   1990   89-29411
[E]—dc20   CIP
                                                          AC

For Nana,
who encouraged me—
and whom I miss dearly.

L.A.K.

For Aunt Gertie

M.R.B.

"Listen, honeybunch," Mom is saying. "I'm really sorry, but I've got a million things to do today. I'm going to have to leave you with your grandmother. She'll be here at nine."

I try not to smile. "Really?"

"We'll do something terrific tomorrow, you and me," says Mom. "Have a picnic in the park, maybe. I was looking forward to today."

So was I, actually. But Nana! Nana and I always have a great time together.

I go upstairs to wait and imagine our day together.

"Hello-o-o-o Natalie Patalie," Nana will call as she drives up to the house. She always calls me Natalie Patalie. She used to call me her chickadee, but she says I've gotten too big for that now.

"What shall we do today?" she'll ask. And she almost always agrees with anything I suggest.

Sometimes we go to the zoo. Nana likes the
seals best.

"Aar, aar," she barks, waddling just like the
seals by their pool. She calls them each by name.
Louis is the biggest, and Nana's favorite. Nana

winks at him, and once he even winked back. We
visit the monkeys next, because they're my
favorite. Nana never minds when I pretend to be
a monkey, and she never rushes me to see the
other animals.

Some days Nana and I go shopping. Nana
poses like the mannequins in the store windows.
Other people stop and watch, but she doesn't
care. "That Nana," says Mom when I tell her,
"a born actress." Sometimes Nana buys me a
dress or a nightgown or a funny T-shirt, and
sometimes she buys a present for Mom or Daddy.

Once I bought Nana a crazy hat, with orange flowers and a toy turtle perched on top. She says all her friends want one now.

One winter day, Nana and I went skating in the park. The lake was completely frozen. Nana taught me how to skate backwards, and when I learned, she gave me purple earmuffs to

celebrate. Back at the house, we drank hot chocolate with marshmallows. Nana loves marshmallows. She never tells me they're "pure sugar."

When it rains, Nana and I have an inside day.
Nana squeezes orange juice from real oranges,
and I get to choose my own little cereal box. Then
we pull out cartons of old pictures from the closet.

Nana shows me pictures of Mom when she was a little girl. She tells me funny stories, like how Mom used to go limp and say "spaghetti arms" whenever Nana tried to put a coat on her to go out. Just like me!

Nana is the one who taught me to dance. She says she and Grampa used to paint the town red.

And she makes better block towers than
anyone I know.

Last summer, Nana broke her arm and I had to take care of her. I painted hearts and daisies on her cast and brought her milk and cookies on a tray. We got crumbs all over the bed, but Nana laughed and said that chocolate chip cookies taste as good *on* the tummy as *in* it.

Nana is the only person I know who has a
friend named Viola.

One afternoon while I was visiting, Viola called
Nana on the telephone. "Come on over!" she said
excitedly. "Henrietta's just had kittens!"

When Nana and I arrived at Viola's, Henrietta was nursing five of the sweetest little kittens you've ever seen. Nana and Viola whispered together, and then Nana nudged me.

"Go, ahead, pick one," she said.
"But Mom—"
"Don't worry about your mom. I'll fix it."

She did, too. In less than six weeks, Freda—
that's Nana's real name, and that's what I named
my kitten—was mine.

I told Nana she was magic. She just said kids
always listen to their mothers, even when the kid
is thirty-five years old.

Sometimes when it's too cold to go outside, Nana lets me try on her lipstick and blush. Once she had a bottle of crazy-colored nail polish, and soon we both had ten blue fingernails and ten blue toenails.

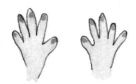

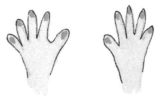

Nana brushes my hair, too, way back off my
face. She calls me her Alice in Wonderland.
Nana says I got my blond hair from her.

"That's right, I've always been a blonde," she
tells me, "and I'll always be one." She pats her
hair happily.

Nana loves *Sesame Street*. She thinks Bert is a hoot.

Nana feeds all the dogs in the neighborhood.
When we go for a walk, she grabs a handful of
biscuits and puts them in her pocketbook. Then

each time we see a dog, she calls, "Here, sport," and throws a biscuit. I used to be scared of dogs, but not anymore.

Nana is always on time. She says when you make a date with someone you care about, it's like a promise. Nana should be here in 5... 4...3...seconds.

Honk, honk.
Nana always keeps her promises.

"Hello-o-o-o Natalie Patalie," I hear her holler from the car. She's wearing a baseball cap.

"Now, Natalie," Mom whispers in my ear, "you be good, and I'll pick you up just the minute I'm done. Can you try to have some fun?"

I see Nana winking at me, waving two baseball tickets in the air.

I smile up at Mom. "Don't worry about me," I tell her, and run down the walk to Nana.